MW01579777

I.M. DEHD

THE BEAST WITH THE RED EAR

TEXT BY VANESSA RAMOS

ILLUSTRATED BY B. SABO
WITH CONTRIBUTING ARTIST COUNTANDRA

STONE ARCH BOOKS
a capstone imprint

Published by Stone Arch Books, an imprint of Capstone
1710 Roe Crest Drive, North Mankato, Minnesota 56003
capstonepub.com

Library of Congress Cataloging-in-Publication Data is
available on the Library of Congress website.

ISBN: 9781669066736 (hardcover)
ISBN: 9781669066866 (paperback)
ISBN: 9781669066842 (eBook PDF)

Summary: To get his little sister to behave while he's
babysitting, Jacob tells her the tale of the Cucuy, a beast
with a red ear that's always listening for naughty children
to make its meal. But Jacob is breaking a few rules himself.
When the monster visits the siblings, can they work together
to escape its clutches?

Designed by Hilary Wacholz

Printed and bound in the USA.   5853

TABLE OF CONTENTS

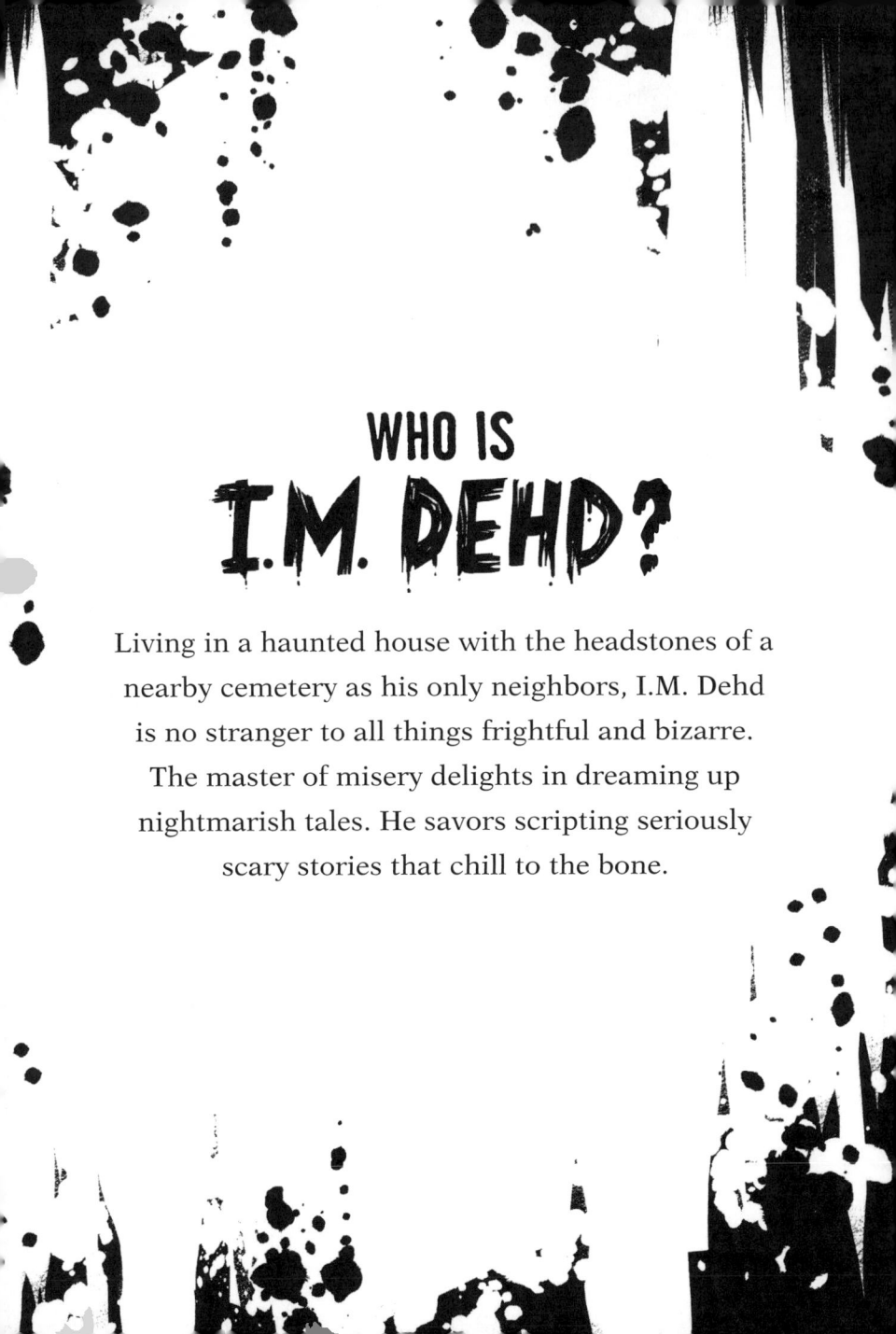

WHO IS
I.M. DEHD?

Living in a haunted house with the headstones of a
nearby cemetery as his only neighbors, I.M. Dehd
is no stranger to all things frightful and bizarre.
The master of misery delights in dreaming up
nightmarish tales. He savors scripting seriously
scary stories that chill to the bone.

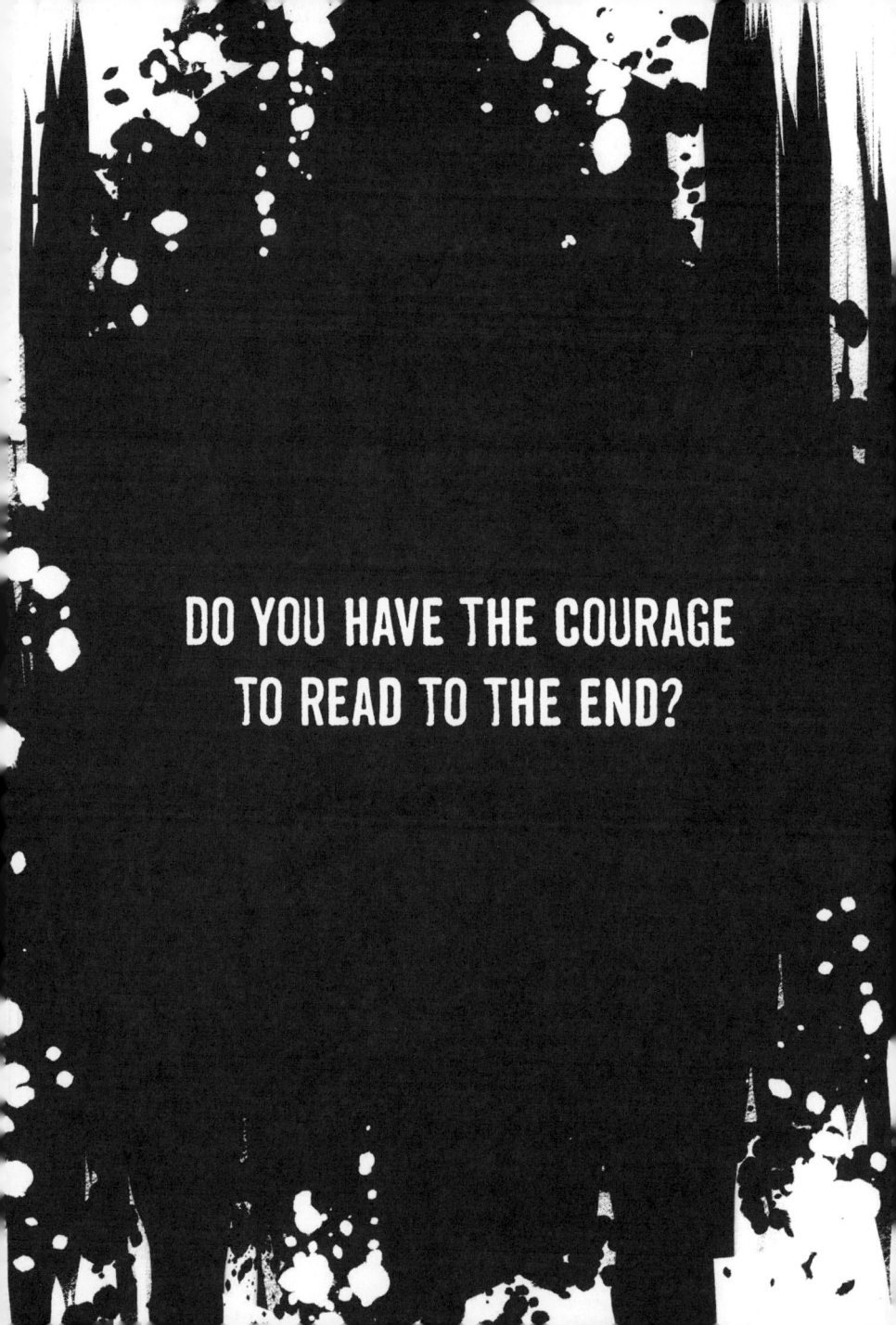

CHAPTER 1

THE BUSINESS OF BABYSITTING

"I need you both on your best behavior," Mami said as she reached for her coat hanging near the front door. "Remember—"

"I know, I know," Jacob interrupted. He finished Mami's sentence. "Take care of my sister. Don't burn the house down."

"And?" Mami asked.

"No video games," Jacob finished.

"That's right." Mami smiled at him. "We're so lucky to have such a responsible babysitter."

From her spot beside their mother, Lola rolled her eyes. Jacob could feel heat rising to his cheeks. He knew his seven-year-old sister was thinking she could take care of herself. Mami and Papi were going to a fancy fundraiser tonight, and this would be Jacob's first time babysitting Lola.

Lola threw her arms around Mami's waist to say goodbye. "Lola," Mami said as she smoothed her hair, "please listen to your brother tonight."

"You know I will, Mami," Lola replied.

She pulled back from the hug. When Mami wasn't looking, she stuck out her tongue at Jacob.

"We'll be okay, Mami," Jacob said. "Promise."

Lola skipped over to the living room couch where she had been making a nest out of blankets.

Mami nodded and sighed. "Make sure to lock up behind me."

Mami pulled the front door open and ran to meet Papi, who was waiting in the car on the driveway. The headlights shone like two bright eyes in the night, watching Jacob.

He shivered. *I'm home,* Jacob thought. *I have nothing to be afraid of.* He quickly closed the door, locked it, then pulled on the handle to double-check it.

Jacob turned around and took in the adultless home. Without Papi cooking up a storm in the kitchen or Mami reading in her chair in the living room, their two-story house suddenly felt empty.

And a little eerie.

Mami had left the lamp on by her chair, and shadows stretched across the carpet and onto the walls. Jacob walked to Lola's nest of blankets on the couch. He gave it a nudge. It was empty.

Great. Where is she hiding? Jacob wondered.

Nothing was funnier to Jacob's sister than a good jump scare. She was always leaping from closets or from behind corners or from anywhere else she could hide. Then she would yell out, "Gotcha!" followed by, "Did I scare you?"

You would think Jacob would be used to it by now, but he was not.

THUMP!

THUMP!

THUMP!

Jacob tensed at the sudden sound. Slowly, he turned toward the stairs.

It was Lola, tromping down, dragging a suitcase behind her with both hands.

She grinned. "Let's play dress-up!"

Jacob grimaced as he ran to help her with the heavy suitcase. Dress-up wasn't much better than dealing with her jump scares.

It's going to be a long night, he thought.

He wished he had known what he was signing up for when he completed "The Business of Babysitting" online course. All Jacob had wanted to do was earn money for a new gaming system. He had taken the course to prove to Mami and Papi that, as a sixth grader, he was ready for the responsibility of watching Lola. His certificate of completion hung on the refrigerator door.

Now Jacob wondered if he should have mowed lawns or washed cars instead. At least he would not have needed to face the prospect of playing dress-up with his kid sister.

"We have to eat dinner first, Lola," Jacob said. "Let's bring this back up to your room."

PING

A notification sounded on Jacob's phone. He balanced the suitcase against his leg and reached into his back pocket to check it.

It was a group text from his gaming friends.

They were trying to convince him to join the *Trials of Terror* video game tournament online tonight.

Jacob ignored the message, stuffed the phone back into his pocket, and heaved the suitcase up the flight of stairs.

"I'm stronger than you are," Lola taunted as she leaped ahead of him. Jacob didn't reply and rolled the suitcase of costumes into her bedroom.

"C'mon, Papi left us some lasagna. Your favorite," Jacob said. He hoped dinner would take long enough that there would be no time left for dress-up.

"I'll race you!" Lola shouted as she bolted down the stairs.

But for a second, Jacob didn't move. He was too shocked by the sound of the front door hinges groaning open and closed.

Jacob scrambled to the entry.

"Hey, watch out!" Lola shouted as he pushed past. "What's your deal?"

Jacob barely heard her as he stared at the open front door. *I swear I locked it*, he thought.

Rookie mistake.

Jacob shut the door and twisted the lock. "Sorry," he told his sister. He forced himself to laugh. "Last one in the kitchen is a rotten egg."

It did not take much to encourage Lola. She was off and running again toward the brightly lit kitchen.

"I won! I won!" Jacob heard Lola cheer as he followed in behind her. He watched her dance around the kitchen island.

Jacob pulled the lasagna out of the fridge. But he had lost his appetite.

Something didn't feel quite right about this night.

CHAPTER 2

YOU'RE THE BOSS

Babysitting was proving to be a tough business.

Although Jacob had hoped dinner would take up a good chunk of time, the whole process had taken longer than he expected. Much longer.

Lola didn't want to eat the lasagna. She didn't want to help clean up. She wanted to know when Mami and Papi would be home. She wanted to wait up for them until midnight. And she definitely did *not* want to get ready for bed.

"We haven't even played dress-up yet. C'mon, Jacob, please," Lola whined from the kitchen floor. She was sprawled out on her back, pouting.

Why is Lola making it so hard for me to do my job? Jacob wondered as he put the last of their dishes in the dishwasher. She never acted this whiny with Mami and Papi around.

"I didn't make the rules, Lola," he said. "You have to be in bed by eight."

Tears welled in Lola's eyes. "You think you're the boss!" she cried.

Before Jacob could protest, Lola was up from the kitchen floor. She stomped back upstairs to her bedroom.

PING

Jacob checked his phone. It was his friends again.

The *Trials of Terror* video game tournament was starting in thirty minutes.

He stared at the screen. He had always wanted to play in one of these tournaments. But Mami and Papi had strict rules about screen time, especially when it came to gaming.

Friday isn't even a school night, though, Jacob thought.

Sure, Mami had reminded him "no video games." But maybe she meant no games while watching Lola.

And who knows when I'll get another chance to play in a tournament, Jacob reasoned. He glanced at the front door, still firmly closed. *And hanging with my friends would help take the creep factor out of being home alone.*

He thought about what Lola had said. He *was* the boss tonight. He could make his own rules, his own decisions.

So Jacob decided: The faster he could get Lola off to dreamland, the sooner he could text his friends and tell them that he would be joining after all.

He slid the phone back into his pocket, determined. "Lola!" he shouted. "Bedtime in five minutes!"

Jacob shut the lights off in the kitchen. He checked the front door again and left Mami's lamp on in the living room.

As he headed for the stairs, the lamplight flickered. A chill crept up his spine. A draft swept past, causing goose bumps to form on his arms.

With a shiver, Jacob bounded up the stairs, taking them two at a time. He was out of breath when he reached the top.

It's just your mind playing tricks on you, Jacob told himself.

He walked quickly toward Lola's bedroom. All was quiet.

He nudged open the door.

The lights were off. A pale blue ribbon of moonlight floated through the window next to his sister's bed. Jacob could make out a Lola-sized shape under the unicorn-themed comforter. He inched closer to make sure she was asleep.

Something creaked behind him.

He paused.

He began to turn around when—

RRRAAAR!

A sudden growl made Jacob stumble backward, hitting his shoulder hard against the bedroom wall.

A dark shape flew out of the closet and straight for him.

CHAPTER 3

STORY TIME

"Gotcha, Jacob Torres!" Lola shouted as she flicked on the bedroom light. She cannonballed into her bed.

Jacob took a deep breath and tried not to let her see that she *had* gotten him.

Now that the lights were on, Jacob could see that Lola had emptied the dress-up suitcase from earlier. Tutus from her old dance recitals were flung across the room. Rubber Halloween masks and costume props littered the floor. She had even pulled on fairy wings over her pajamas.

"You said get ready for bed, so I did," Lola said proudly.

Playing dress-up is not what I meant, Jacob thought.

"Stuffies," Lola demanded as she snuggled under her covers.

Jacob glared at his sister and tossed stuffed animals at her one by one, a little harder than he should.

Jacob checked the time on his phone. He had fifteen minutes left until game time. Jacob decided to tell Lola a bedtime story. One told to him by his old babysitter.

One that would keep her in bed.

"Lola, have you ever heard of the Cucuy?" Jacob asked.

"Who's the Cu—" Lola began, but Jacob clamped his hand over her mouth before she could finish.

Jacob whispered, "You don't say the name more than three times in a row if you can help it. Let's just call it the Beast with the Red Ear."

He leaned in closer. "The beast is an ancient monster. It has a big, hairy body. It has rows and rows of razor-sharp teeth. But most noticeable of all? It has a huge red ear. It's always listening for misbehaving children. The ear grows brighter and bigger as children break rules. And the more you act out, the hungrier the beast becomes. It gets hungrier and hungrier until all it wants is to eat your flesh and bones . . ."

Lola pulled her favorite stuffie closer.

"And getting a meal is easy," Jacob continued. "The beast just crawls out of its dark, dank lair. Then it shape-shifts to find its way into any home. It can trap children by mimicking the voices of people who love them, or it simply snatches kids from their beds at night."

Jacob paused. "Y'know . . . years ago, I wasn't listening to my sitter either. I didn't want to go to sleep. I was lying in bed when it felt like someone—or *something*—was sitting on my chest. It must have weighed at least a thousand pounds. And the *stench*. Ugh. Like a sewer pipe had burst. I slowly opened my eyes."

"That's when I saw it. The Beast with the Red Ear. Drool dripped from its fangs as it opened its big and terrible mouth and hissed, 'Behave.'"

Lola was as white as her bedsheets now. "*What?!* No way that happened," she said. "Why didn't you scream for help? Where did the Cu— I mean, Beast with the Red Ear go? Why didn't he eat you?"

Jacob sat up straight and shrugged. "All I know is that from that moment on, I became the best-behaved kid *ever*," he replied. "And the beast never came back."

Jacob had meant to scare only his sister with the story. But he felt his heart racing.

That was because he hadn't been making up that last part. It was all true. Whether the Cucuy's visit had been real or a nightmare, he wasn't sure. Either way, though, a shiver ran through him as he remembered that night.

Maybe that's why I'm so jumpy, Jacob realized. *Some part of me must still believe the Cucuy can get me, even though I haven't seen it since.*

Jacob felt shaky as he rose from the corner of Lola's bed. He stretched, faked a yawn, and told his sister to go to sleep.

As he turned to leave, he thought he heard Lola's curtains rustle.

Jacob tensed and quickly looked around. Nothing appeared out of the ordinary. There wasn't the telltale stench of the Cucuy. Lola's room smelled like cotton candy.

I really need to stop freaking myself out, Jacob thought.

Still, his hand shook as he pulled the door closed behind him.

That was when Lola screamed.

"THE CUCUY!"

CHAPTER 1

SAFE AND SOUND ON THE JOB?

Jacob acted without thinking. All he could picture was the Cucuy drooling over Lola, ready to have her as an evening snack. He leaned into the door as he pushed it open, stumbling into his sister's room.

But the only monster Jacob could see was Lola.

She was still sitting in the middle of her bed. Now, though, she wore a big grin and was clutching her stomach, holding in laughter.

"Gotcha again, Jacob Torres!" Lola shouted.

Jacob's heart felt like it was in his ears, pounding. He took one, two, three breaths. Then he issued a final warning, "Go to sleep now, Lola, or you'll see that the Cucuy will get you after all."

Jacob couldn't help it.

He slammed the door behind him.

Jacob tromped across the hall from Lola's room and into his gaming sanctuary. Unlike Lola's room, his was as neat as a pin. Jacob texted his friends to let them know he was signing in. He could feel a sense of calm flow back into his body as he picked up the controller. At least Lola's antics hadn't cost him any game time.

28

The *Trials of Terror* logo filled his computer screen. Jacob felt a twinge of guilt. Any gaming that night was technically off-limits. But he wasn't actually allowed to *ever* play this particular game.

I'm not breaking Mami's rules, he reasoned. *I'm just making new ones. I can do that because I'm in charge this evening.*

Lola was another story. *She* had caused tons of trouble. She hadn't listened to Jacob as Mami had told her. She had thrown a tantrum, destroyed her room, and refused to go to bed.

If the Cucuy *was* real, and if it came . . . it would definitely take her first.

Not that Jacob wanted that.

As he navigated the login screen, he relaxed even more, enjoying the way the letters chimed when he selected them. When he hit Enter, he did a double take.

Was it a glitch in his screen, or had he seen a hard glint of red?

Jacob pushed off one side of his headset. He couldn't help but think he was like the Cucuy, listening with one ear for his misbehaving sister.

And she delivered.

THUD

The sound was unmistakable. It was as if Lola had rolled out of bed and onto the floor.

Probably slithering down the hall on her belly to scare me again, he thought.

Jacob sighed and messaged the other players that he'd be back.

"This is the last time," Jacob muttered as he headed to Lola's room.

He flung open the door. Her bed was empty.

Wow. What a surprise, he thought. *Another prank.*

WHAM!

The door slammed shut on its own.

Except there was no Lola cannonballing past him.

Jacob sniffed the air.

The cotton candy smell was gone. Instead, Jacob caught a whiff of something rotten. Almost like . . . sewage and pond scum.

He had smelled that smell before.

"Lola?" Jacob rasped as if his vocal cords had stopped working.

His eyes darted around the room.

They locked on to a large red ear pulsing from the side of a misshapen head. The monster lurked by the window next to Lola's empty bed.

"You're b-b-back," Jacob stuttered.

A slow smile stretched across the face of the Beast with the Red Ear. Then it leaped toward Jacob with its claws outstretched.

And the world went black.

CHAPTER 5

SAFETY FIRST

Jacob blinked open his eyes. An inky darkness surrounded him. A cold damp licked at his skin. He shuddered as a draft swept over him, carrying that awful stench.

Don't panic. Don't panic, he told himself.

As his eyes adjusted to the darkness, he could make out toothlike spikes reaching down from above. *Stalactites? Is that what they're called?* He remembered learning about them in science class. So he must be in a cave, underground. Somewhere dark and dank just like in the Cucuy legend. The legend that had proven to be one hundred percent true.

Jacob shuddered. The last thing he remembered was the beast leaping at him.

But what happened next? he wondered. *Did I pass out? Why did the Cucuy drag me to its lair? I wasn't misbehaving!*

Jacob shook his aching head, trying to sort out his thoughts. He was so groggy, and everything ached.

Something hard and pointed pressed into his side. When Jacob shifted, a clatter echoed through the dark cave. He slowly reached for his phone, inching his fingers into his pocket. Jacob turned on the flashlight, but he immediately wished he had kept it off.

He was sitting on a pile of old bones.

Jacob tried not to heave. But the jolt of panic cleared his brain fog.

Lola! he realized in a rush. She hadn't been in her room. The Cucuy must have taken her too! Where was she?

Jacob circled the small light around the cavern. He had a duty to uphold as a babysitter and brother—and that was to take care of his sister.

I need to get off of these bones, and I need to find her, he thought. *Fast.*

The beam from his phone revealed more cave formations. Golden, toothlike spikes hung from the ceiling, and green-speckled spikes also rose from all over the ground. Stalagmites.

Stay on the bone pile, or jump off and risk getting stabbed? Jacob wondered. *Lots of tough choices today.*

For some reason, the first rule from Jacob's babysitting course floated into his mind: Do not accept jobs you can't handle.

"The Business of Babysitting" should have prepared me for monsters and how to escape their lairs, Jacob laughed to himself.

If he didn't laugh, he was sure he would cry.

Jacob took a deep breath and held up his phone's flashlight again. This time he moved the light slowly across the walls. He spotted a long ledge. It was wide enough to hold a small girl.

Jacob kept the light steady, studying the ledge in case Lola was tucked away in the deep shadows. But he didn't see anything.

Instead, he heard a sound. It was between a chirp and a squeak. A massive black form swooped toward him.

Bats!

Jacob ducked from the swarm of flying bats overhead. The movement caused the pile of bones to give way.

CRRRRRASH!

The bones rattled and rolled as Jacob tumbled onto the cold and slimy cave floor. His phone hit one of the stalagmites, but the light kept shining. He scrambled toward it on his hands and knees, frantically pushing past bones. He grabbed the phone, found his footing, and stood tall.

Figure out a way down from the bone pile? Check. Thanks, bats, Jacob joked nervously. *I'd better keep moving. Don't wanna wait and see if all that racket reminded the Cucuy of its dinner.*

"Could you be any louder?"

Jacob's ears perked up in surprise at the sound of the exasperated voice. It echoed throughout the cavern.

"Lola?" Jacob asked.

"Where are you?" Lola's question rang in the air.

Jacob hesitated. *I know now that the legend of the Cucuy is true. So . . . how can I know if that is really Lola? What if it's just the beast mimicking her voice?*

"Jacob," Lola's voice quavered.

"Marco?" he finally called.

"Polo," the voice replied.

The voice was unmistakably Lola's.

There was no way a hundreds-of-years-old monster had played this game of swimming pool tag.

"Marco," Jacob repeated. He scrambled past a few stalagmites. Each time Lola responded with "Polo" to his "Marco" call, he moved again.

Slow but steady wins the race, Jacob told himself as he navigated the strange, shadowy terrain of the cave.

Lola's voice led him into a larger, cooler space. Sure enough, his phone's flashlight revealed his sister. She was sitting in the center of the cavern on a gigantic slab of stone, rubbing her arms to keep warm in her thin pajamas. It felt like he had hiked miles to reach her.

"Where are we?" Lola croaked as he rushed over. Her big, brown eyes filled with tears.

"In trouble," Jacob said. He hugged her hard.

His relief at finding his sister, though, was short-lived.

"Way to get us taken, Jacob," she hissed, pulling away.

"Me?" Jacob fumed.

"Yeah. I bet you were playing video games," Lola replied. "You broke Mami's rules and so the Cu— Beast with the Red Ear came."

"*You* were the one who wasn't going to bed!" Jacob replied, although he could feel his face getting hot from guilt. "You weren't listening to me all evening!"

"Why should I listen to you?" Her voice grew louder and ricocheted off the walls of the cavern.

A flutter of wings sounded above them.

"*Shhhhh,* Lola!" Jacob said in a hushed voice. "We don't want to draw more attention from the beast, do we? Or bats? Right now we need to work together and find a way out of here."

Lola crossed her arms and turned her back on Jacob. She still had on her fairy wings. One wing was crushed against her shoulder blade.

"Fine. Let's go that way then," she finally said, pointing the direction Jacob had come from.

"I don't think that's a good idea," Jacob said. The last thing he wanted was to revisit the pile of bones. Or for Lola to see their possible fate.

Lola whipped around. "Well, I think it is."

The ground rumbled beneath their feet.

"Whoa. Did you feel that?" Jacob flashed the light from his phone downward.

"What are you looking at? Let me see," Lola said. She grabbed for the phone, accidentally knocking it from his hand.

The light went out as the phone crashed to the ground.

Jacob groaned. "Great, Lola. Now you've really done it!"

Without the phone's flashlight, complete
and total darkness pressed down on them like
a weighted blanket. But it was anything but
comforting.

"What are we going to do, what are
we going to do . . ." Jacob fumed in the
pitch-black cavern. He paused. "Lola?"

"I'm over here."

"Yeah, because I can really see you in—"

A deep growl echoing in the distance
cut Jacob off. The ground rumbled again as
he caught a whiff of *that* stench, filling the
cavern.

CHAPTER 6

IN AN EMERGENCY...

The smell of sewage was a sure sign that the Cucuy was near and ready for its meal.

There's no time to be angry, Jacob thought. *We need to get out of here. Now!*

Jacob crouched down and swept his hand against the dark cave floor. "Quick, Lola. See if you can find my phone."

"Gross," Lola whispered from somewhere beside him. "What is that smell? And why is the floor so slimy?"

As if on cue, the ground rumbled for a third time. The force was enough to knock Jacob and Lola down onto their knees. Either this cave was alive, or the Beast with the Red Ear was moving toward them.

From this lower position, though, Jacob saw something. A glimmer in the distance.

"Lola, I think we have a way out," he said, his heart beating fast. "This cave is probably a whole series of connected underground spaces, right? Like that one we visited in Forestville? I can see a light, and I bet it's from a space farther away. One that leads to outside."

I just hope my eyes aren't playing tricks on me, Jacob thought.

"I see it too!" Lola whispered.

"Then stay close and start crawling," he said.

Jacob began scooting forward. It was slow going, but at least since he was already on

the ground, he didn't have to worry about tripping in the dark.

That was when his knee landed on something hard.

CRACK

Jacob groaned. *Pretty sure that was the sound of my phone's screen breaking,* he realized. He reached under his knee. *Yep.*

Jacob felt around for the power button. *Please work, please work, please work,* he chanted in his head.

It took a few frantic tries, but despite the broken screen, the phone whirred back to life. Jacob wished he could just call for help, but there was no signal. He tapped the flashlight icon, and a steady beam of light lit up their surroundings once again.

"Lola, we're back in business!" Jacob leaped to his feet. "You ready to book it?"

Lola scrambled up from the ground. "Ready!"

They started to run, slipping and sliding along the slick cave floor. Jacob could not tell if the pond scum smell was coming from the cave walls dripping with moisture, or if it was the stench of the Cucuy. He wasn't about to wait and see.

Jacob held up his phone as they ran, but the light was only bright enough to fight the darkness off a few feet in front of them. The rumbling underfoot continued as the siblings hurried through the dark and damp—until Lola suddenly stopped in her tracks.

"My legs hurt," she said. "I can't run anymore." Her chest heaved, and she placed her hands on her knees.

"You can do this, Lola," Jacob replied. "Not much farther."

"Easy for you to say. You have longer legs!" Lola said between breaths.

Jacob decided to try another tactic to get his sister moving. After all, "The Business of Babysitting" class encouraged sitters to listen when kids shared their feelings.

"I know you're tired right now, Lola, and I'm glad you told me," he said.

"Really?"

"Really."

It was hard to determine distance in the dark, but the sliver of light had become a soft, orange glow. It gently lit up the walls around them. All Jacob could think about was how it meant they would soon be home. Mami and Papi would tell them about the fundraiser. They would all laugh together in the warm comfort of the kitchen.

"We have to keep moving, okay? We're so close to getting out of here!" Jacob pointed in excitement at the orange glow. "We don't even need the flashlight anymore."

He pocketed his phone. He held out his hand to Lola.

She hesitated. Then, she took it.

Her brow furrowed in determination. "Okay."

They started to run again, silently. Jacob was glad for this moment of quiet between them. Not peace, just quiet. It made him wonder what life would be like if they got along instead. If they made it out of this mess, maybe they would be able to find out.

In their rush to exit the cave, Jacob and Lola didn't notice the sudden slope in the ground up ahead.

"*AAAHHH!*" Jacob cried as his feet slipped out from under him.

Still holding hands, the siblings lost their balance and fell onto their backs. They screamed as they both began sliding down the slick, steep slope. Jacob tried to slow them by anchoring his feet in front of him, but his heels wouldn't catch.

Please let this be the scariest shortcut ever, Jacob thought. He watched the orange light grow brighter. *We're almost home. We have to be.*

Jacob and Lola tumbled onto level ground.

The light they had been running—and then sliding—toward wasn't from an outdoor source. It was a large fire, its tall flames lighting up a cavern.

It was not a way out as Jacob had hoped.

CHAPTER 7

HAVE A PLAN

The flames of the fire burned bright, and the smell of smoke mixed with *that* stench reminded Jacob of rotting meat. Rough-hewn logs had been arranged within a large circle of stones in the center of the chamber. An iron rack stood next to the fire. It had a handle at the end of what looked like a big fork.

Jacob had seen something like that iron rack before, when Papi roasted a pig for a family reunion. He guessed this contraption was also used for roasting. But not pigs.

The siblings got to their feet, taking in the small, well-lit chamber. Jacob was at least thankful he and Lola weren't hurt from their fall. He looked over his shoulder at the narrow tunnel. They couldn't go back the way they had come. The passageway was too steep and slick to climb.

This is worse than being in the bone room, Jacob decided. *Much, much worse.*

A deep growl shook the chamber. It was louder than the ones Jacob had heard earlier.

Closer.

Lola gasped and clamped her hands over her mouth. Her eyes widened in disbelief.

Jacob followed her gaze across the fire to another tunnel on the opposite side of the chamber.

Claws grasped the edge of the tunnel entrance. A massive arm emerged as the thing pulled its head through the opening, revealing the distinct glow of a red ear.

The Cucuy slumped onto the cave floor. Its giant body was covered in coarse fur that looked like thousands of short porcupine quills. The beast was carrying more wood for the fire. Its right hind leg dragged as it grunted and shuffled across the space.

Jacob quickly tugged Lola behind a rocky outcrop to get out of view. But something in the way the Cucuy paused and cocked its head to the side caught Jacob's attention.

Then Jacob realized: The monster wasn't using its sight. The beast's beady eyes lolled around in their sockets. Unfocused. It was navigating by sound—with its giant red ear.

It can't see us, Jacob thought. *It can only listen for us.*

Jacob saw this fact register on Lola's face too.

She met Jacob's gaze and pointed at her ear. Then she moved a finger in front of her lips as if she was saying, "*Shhhh.*"

Jacob did the same to let her know he understood.

The Cucuy couldn't find them if they were quiet, if they were getting along and cooperating.

If they were *behaving*.

Jacob and Lola used to play games together all the time. But when Jacob had entered middle school and schedules got busier, family game nights came to an end. One of their favorite games had been charades. They had to act out words or phrases using gestures. Jacob and Lola had always beaten Mami and Papi. It was one thing they were good at doing together.

It was time to put those skills to work.

Lola made a circle in the air and pointed to the fire.

Location! Jacob thought.

Lola pointed to herself, pretended to yell, then pointed at the Cucuy. She then pointed to Jacob and made a motion as if pushing someone.

Jacob could only suspect that someone would be the Cucuy. He pointed to himself, the beast, and then the fire. Lola tapped her index finger against her nose and pointed to Jacob—the signal he was right.

It was Jacob's turn to add onto their scheme. He pointed toward the tunnel the Cucuy had come from and made a running motion with his fingers. Lola nodded.

They had silently made their plan. Lola would jump out and scare the Beast with the Red Ear. That would be Jacob's chance to push it into the fire. Then they would take the tunnel, which seemed to be the only way out of this chamber.

Now, they needed to get into position.

And they needed their plan to work.

CHAPTER 8

TAKE CHARGE

The chamber was filled with cave formations that looked like flowing water, only frozen. Jacob motioned for Lola to move behind the one nearest to the fire. From there, they would put their plan into action.

Jacob's and Lola's eyes remained fixed on the beast as they inched their way around the chamber toward the formation, careful not to make a sound. The Cucuy's head remained cocked to one side, but its ear was starting to pulsate. It was as if it had a sense of their growing mischief.

There wasn't much time, and Jacob knew it.

Jacob silently urged Lola along the few feet that remained. She moved faster, only to trip over a loose rock on the cave floor.

Jacob reached out to keep her from falling. His hand just grazed her arm.

Lola let out a small yelp as she landed hard near the iron rack.

The Cucuy's head snapped left, angling its ear in their direction. It pressed its giant hands against the cave floor. Its yellowed nails scraped against the limestone, leaving deep grooves.

SCRRRREEECH!

Jacob held his breath. On the ground, Lola stayed frozen.

But the Cucuy didn't move either. The beast was alert. Yet it had not been able to pinpoint their location.

Jacob felt relief flood through him.

Lola silently scrambled back toward the chamber wall and behind the flowstone. Her fairy wings were tattered now. She peeked out at Jacob and gave him a thumbs-up, even though she was as white as a ghost.

The Cucuy sniffed and snorted and continued to listen.

Its ear was growing brighter and larger.

Jacob inched closer toward the flowstone to join Lola. She was staring at the beast intently. She pulled herself into a crouch, as if she was about to jump.

I'm not in the right spot yet! Jacob thought in panic. He tried to catch Lola's eye to silently tell her to wait and stick to the plan.

But before he could, Lola leaped from behind the flowstone and into the direct path of the Beast with the Red Ear. She shouted:

RRRAAAR!

The Cucuy snarled in surprise. It opened its mouth wide, revealing rows of teeth like a barracuda.

Jacob didn't have any time to think. He sprinted forward.

The beast snapped its jaws just as Jacob dove at Lola's feet, pushing her out of the way of the monster's bite.

This was not going to plan.

Jacob had to improvise.

He jumped to his feet as the Cucuy shuffled over. He lifted the iron fork from the rack and swung it at the Cucuy. Jacob's aim wasn't perfect, but it was good enough.

The fork caught the tip of the beast's red ear.

Lola scuttled behind Jacob as the Cucuy shrieked. It swayed back and forth, clutching its head. The Cucuy staggered toward the flames as it struggled to find its balance. Jacob and Lola positioned themselves behind it.

This was their chance.

They lunged head-on at the Cucuy and together pushed it into the fire.

The flames flared and raged, and soon all that remained was the shrinking red ear of the beast.

CHAPTER 9

TIME FOR BED

The light drained from the chamber as the flames went down. For a moment, all was silent.

"We did it! We did it! Our plan worked!" Lola shouted, skipping around the chamber.

Jacob shook his head in disbelief. He held his hand up for a high five as Lola circled back to him. She jumped up to hit it.

"Guess you're doing okay then, Lola?" Jacob asked shakily.

"I'm ready for bed," she replied.

Jacob couldn't help but laugh. "At last!"

He looked at the dying fire. He had watched enough movies to know that monsters like the Cucuy sometimes came back. If anything, he hoped that the Cucuy's burnt ear would make it harder to hear smaller arguments and misbehaviors. Still . . .

"What's the next part of the plan?" Lola asked.

Jacob shrugged. "You can be the boss now. What do you think?"

"I think we should get out of this lair," Lola said. She turned and pointed to the tunnel they had watched the Cucuy emerge from.

Jacob smiled and handed Lola his phone. She used the flashlight to guide them out of the darkened chamber.

The tunnel ceiling was low, making the space feel claustrophobic. It reminded Jacob of a subway station. But he would take a tight space over being the Cucuy's dinner. He shuddered at how close they had come, all because of Lola's bad behavior.

No. That's not right, Jacob corrected himself. *It wasn't just Lola's fault. I broke Mami and Papi's rules too.*

"Lola," he said as they shuffled through the tunnel, "we need to keep getting along. Even once we get out of here. That way, the Cucuy won't be able to hear us. It won't be able to come back for us."

"You think he still can?" Lola asked.

"I definitely don't want to risk it," Jacob replied.

Lola nodded. "Then let's promise to be on our best behavior, as Mami would say."

Lola held her finger up for a pinky swear. Jacob hooked his finger with hers and shook it up and down like a handshake.

Jacob and Lola took turns holding the flashlight as they climbed through tight spots in the twisting tunnel. Eventually, they emerged from the underground cave. The tunnel had brought them to the edge of a pond in the woods near their house.

Jacob took a deep breath of the fresh night air. It was dark, but they knew these woods. Soon, they had walked down the moonlit trail right to their house.

Using the spare key hidden in a fake rock, they entered through the back door. It was quiet inside. Mami and Papi weren't back yet.

Jacob looked at the microwave clock in the kitchen. It read 11:30. He couldn't believe only a few hours had passed. It had felt like forever.

Jacob elbowed Lola gently. "We're home. You got us here."

Lola smiled shyly. "We did it together."

"Well, who knew your love of jump scares would come in handy?" Jacob joked. "Especially in besting the beast of legends."

"*I* knew," Lola teased.

Jacob laughed. He had been in a different *Trials of Terror* tournament that night, and both he and Lola had come out champions.

He took in the quiet moment. The lamp in the living room was still giving off a warm glow. The stench that had filled the house earlier was gone.

He and his sister were safe.

The house was in one piece.

But they were filthy. They had soot on their faces and grime and slime on their clothes.

And they had only thirty minutes to clean themselves up and get their clothes in the laundry before Mami and Papi returned.

Because I have no idea how I'd ever explain any of this, Jacob thought.

"Lola, how's this for a plan? Quick showers, fresh clothes, pick up the dress-up clothes in your room, and then get into bed," he said. "Sound good?"

Lola nodded and raced upstairs.

Wow, no pushback, Jacob marveled, following behind her. *She's really staying true to our pinky promise.*

Jacob was showered and dressed long before Lola. So, he began gathering his sister's scattered dress-up costumes and props.

"I can help," Lola volunteered, rushing out of her bathroom smelling like cotton candy. She swooped up the last of the items and handed them to Jacob. Then she folded her tattered fairy wings and placed them in the suitcase herself.

As Jacob closed the suitcase, Lola jumped into bed again.

"Stuffies," she demanded. Jacob tossed a few stuffed animals her way. Gently this time.

"Do you want a story?" Jacob asked.

Lola shook her head quickly. "No more stories for a while. At least not scary ones."

JHUNK

Jacob heard the lock slide in the front door. *Mami and Papi!* he realized. *They're home!*

"Quick, pretend you're asleep," Jacob whispered to his sister.

But Mami moved faster than any monster. She was already up the stairs before Jacob had time to turn off Lola's bedroom light.

"Still up?" Mami asked as she stood in the open doorway. She arched her eyebrow and smiled at both of them. "You two must have had a packed evening. I hope the Cucuy doesn't get you for not going to bed before midnight."

Lola and Jacob exchanged a nervous glance and laughed.

GLOSSARY

CLAUSTROPHOBIC (klah-struh-FOH-bik)—causing fear or worry because a space is narrow, small, and tight

DANK (DANGK)—slightly wet in a way that does not feel good

EXASPERATED (ig-ZAS-puh-rey-tid)—being very annoyed or frustrated

GRIMACE (GRIM-uhs)—to make an expression where your face is twisted up, done because you don't like something

IMPROVISE (IM-pruh-vahyz)—to act without any plan and decide what to do in the moment

INTENTLY (in-TENT-lee)—with great focus

MIMIC (MIM-ik)—to copy

MISCHIEF (MIS-chif)—little tricks or actions that annoy and break the rules in small ways

NAVIGATE (NAV-uh-geyt)—to make one's way through, getting from one point to another

PULSATE (PUHL-seyt)—to throb or move steadily and with a beat, like a pulsing heart

STENCH (STENCH)—a strong, bad smell

DIG DEEPER

1. Do you think telling scary stories to frighten people into behaving a certain way works? Why or why not?

2. How did the text foreshadow, or hint, that something bad would happen while Jacob was babysitting? Look back through the first chapters and find at least three examples.

3. Which moment did you find the scariest in this tale? What made it so scary?

4. Jacob gets annoyed with his sister, but he still cares for her. Think about when you get mad at a sibling or friend. Describe how you work through the frustrated feelings.

5. Write two paragraphs comparing Jacob and Lola's relationship at the start of the story to the end. What caused any changes?

6. At the end, Jacob thinks there is a chance the Cucuy will return. Imagine the beast does come back. Will it go after the Torres siblings, or will it try to snatch up new naughty kids? Can it be defeated for good? Write a sequel to this adventure.

READ THEM ALL!

OBEY THE EGG

TERROR FROM BEYOND THE MIRROR

THE BEAST WITH THE RED EAR

WAITING IN THE WAVES